PIER PAOLO PASOLINI

THE SAVAGE FATHER

Translation and Afterword by Pasquale Verdicchio

D1479354

GUERNICA
TORONTO·BUFFALO·LANCASTER (U.K.)
1999

Original title: *Il padre selvaggio*
Published in 1975 by Giulio Einaudi editore s.p.a., Torino, Italy.
Copyright © 1999, by The Estate of Pier Paolo Pasolini.
Translation and Afterword © 1999, by Pasquale Verdicchio
and Guernica Editions Inc.

Antonio D'Alfonso, editor
Guernica Editions Inc.
P.O. Box 117, Station P, Toronto (ON), Canada M5S 2S6
2250 Military Road, Tonawanda, N.Y. 14150-6000 U.S.A.
Gazelle, Falcon House, Queen Square, Lancaster LA1 1RN U.K.
Printed in Canada.

Legal Deposit — Fourth Quarter
National Library of Canada
Library of Congress Catalog Card Number: 99-64481.

Canadian Cataloguing in Publication Data
Pasolini, Pier Paolo, 1922-1975
The savage father
(Drama series ; 18)
Translation of : Il padre selvaggio.
ISBN 1-55071-081-8
I. Verdicchio, Pasquale, 1954- II. Title. III. Series.
PQ4835.A48P313 1999 852'.914 C99-900887-0

The Savage Father

1. Street School Kado. Exterior Day.

Across a gathering of huts, of mahogany, the teacher arrives at the school. It's the first day. Trembling, inner voice that speaks, etc. He hears shouting — "Brother, brother!" — as the young men call to each other while they play soccer on a funereally pink field in front of the school huts.

The teacher stops to listen to those young men who, as they play with the awkwardness of peasants, ask each other for the ball by shouting: "Brother, brother!"

2. Classroom Kado. Interior Day.

Inner voice speaks: unexplainable happiness at being there, with "Africa's pink" all around. The teacher watches his black students, and is invaded by that exalting inner voice: his idealism, his "poetic state."

3. Classroom Kado. Interior Day. A Little Later.

The teacher's introductory remarks to his students: "One must after all begin to talk. Let's pretend that I have before me last year's white students during the year back home." He speaks, with the confidence of his somewhat childish character and his democratic ideology. But his young men appear to reject such approaches: a tone of improvised friendliness. With his slightly indiscreet (and overly emotional) questions, hoping that the young men might speak, the teacher ends up getting into a slightly embarrassing situation, with no apparent way out. The students neither intend, nor do they know how, to display the sense of their naked "privacy" to this stranger so predisposed with affection and interest for them.

So, with a sudden impulse, the teacher, a little hysterical, and speaking in fits and starts, puts his own "privacy" on display. He gives the ideal reasons as to why he is there, his political convictions, his idealistic vocation (with its faults, etc.): his departure, his arrival at Kado, two days earlier, by plane, etc.

He cannot think of anything better to do than reveal his "problems" to his students. Foremost is the difficulty of his relationship with them: he knows nothing of Africa, only what he has gathered from books. He knows nothing of them, of their families, of their thoughts; nothing, nothing.

The students do not seem shaken by that sincerity, by that confession. They stare at him absentmindedly, defensively: and sweetly, of course, much too sweetly.

Then the teacher begins a lesson that is more sociology than literature, on the origins of Latin poetry (Nevio, Ennio, etc.).

4. Classroom School Kado. Interior Day. The Following Day.

The following day the teacher tries some questions from the previous day's lesson in Latin literature. No one knows how to answer: he questions four, five, six. Every one is either silent or mumbles. Sweet, always, sweet in silence, in mortification, in hostility.

The eyes of one student.

A sad black young man, with tormented eyes . . . Immobile at his desk, a black flower set into the blinding whiteness of his shirt.

Davidson 'Ngibuini, that is his name. The teacher calls on him and, unlike the others, Davidson speaks. But his answer on Ennio and Nevio is an absurd little recital, obviously learned by heart or almost. It is a series of banal and academic information out of some ancient school textbook.

The teacher listens in astonishment. Then, in his idealistic ingenuity, the instinctive delusion quickly transforms into indignation.

He is not angry with Davidson in particular, the sad young man with tormented eyes. He is angry with the previous teachers, colonialists. He is angry with colonialism itself, with neo-colonialism, part and parcel of the most stupid and dangerous conformisms of the European bourgeoisie, etc.

"You are free, you are free!" he tells them loudly. They listen stupefied and silent.

5. Road School Kado. Exterior Day. The Following Day.

The teacher walks along the path between huts and mahoganies, toward the school barracks. The inner voice of his problems persecutes him.

The loud "Brother, brother!" of the young men who wait for the day to begin by playing soccer.

6. Classroom School Kado. Interior Day.

The teacher enters, looks around.

A desk is empty, Davidson's desk.

Offended, traumatized by the teacher's ire — which he though was all directed at him — Davidson did not come to school. The teacher comes to know of it through the unrelated and almost hostile information of the other students. He knows that it is serious, a "precedent" that cannot be set, it cannot be, and needs to be quickly resolved.

So he leaves the classroom, suddenly, more and more absurd, etc.

7. SCHOOL KADO. INTERIOR-EXTERIOR DAY.

Courtyard. Barracks and dormitories. The school at Kado is also a sort of poor "college." The interns, come here from distant tribal homes — reside here.

The teacher goes out to search for Davidson: through the reddish courtyards . . . the mortuary umbrellas of mangoes . . . The kitchen, with the black servants who, during the break hour, laugh like children . . . The dormitories, with the humble luggage of the "interns": white cotton clothes in disorder . . . the odd newspaper . . . some musical instruments . . . a photo here and there at the head of a bed: the father, the mother, with their horrible almost bestial smiles, in some corner of Africa, against their shack . . . against the stores, some shops with black children straggling and laughing.

Davidson is seated down there, where the school's open space ends with a sort of woods, splendid but infertile growth.

The teacher approaches him.

Dialogue between the two. First useless attempts by the teacher, with the usual methods of persuasion. But Davidson is enclosed within the mysterious offense, in his obscure trauma.

Only through desperate means, eventually, the teacher is able to convince him: playing a little bit of the clown, imitating an old black man who speaks Davidson's dialect, which the teacher knows only poorly, therefore causing the young man to smile.

8. CLASSROOM SCHOOL KADO. INTERIOR DAY. A FEW DAYS
    LATER.

The teacher looks his students over.

Nothing has changed. The inner voice signals him desperately, passionately.

He tries to repeat the lesson on Ennio, interrupting it every now and then to ask someone what they have understood, if they understand the sense of some of his words, if some of the concepts are new. Event by event, word by word, concept by concept, the young men understand. But they cannot grasp the cultural thread that the teacher is pursuing. The methodology through which he addresses things in a way so different from what the students' "colonial" teachers had accustomed them to expect.

They know nothing of what goes on in the world outside of the things they learn in school.

"But which books, aside from your textbooks, which books have you read?"

They haven't read a thing, they have never owned a book; the College has a ridiculous library.

9. CLASSROOM SCHOOL KADO. INTERIOR DAY. A FEW DAYS LATER.

Since things already consecrated by teaching, traditional things, concepts rendered a-prioristic by school, have become taboo in the minds of the young men, undetractable, the teacher thinks about connecting with their sensibility through a real relationship through some not strictly pedagogical methods.

Something outside of the set curriculum.

And he begins — with the slightly scandalous tone that characterizes his idealism, always a little naive and out-of-step — to read, in class, the work of a contemporary black poet (Senghor, for example, or De Andrade, etc.).

It is a difficult poetry: the cultural product of refined European schools (from Dylan Thomas on down to Symbolism), and therefore difficult to approach stylistically. In addition, the content is equally difficult, because it is the product of an ideology that mixes progressivism and nationalism, laicism and claims of the ancestral spirit. The young men understand their own poet even less than they do Ennio or Nevio, so the teacher takes on the task of paraphrasing it, explaining it verse by verse, *image by image.* And he renders the images familiar for the young men, using those that they experience every day, during the course of their daily life in Kado.

9. A, B, C, D, E, F, G, H, I, J, K, L, M, N

Environments described by the poetry, city of Kado and forest. *(Poem.)*

10. STREET SCHOOL KADO. EXTERIOR DAY. A FEW WEEKS LATER.

This time the teacher arrives at the school barracks with news. He carries a large and heavy package on his shoulders. Two little children who trot along behind him, carry two more large and heavy packages.

The young men who are there playing soccer gather around their teacher. For the first time — like their fathers, who ran to greet the white men who brought naive gifts — their curiosity causes them to be more familiar with their teacher.

They help him carry the heavy packages into the classroom . . .

11. CLASSROOM SCHOOL KADO. INTERIOR DAY.

The packages are opened in class. They are full of books, hundreds of books that the teacher has ordered from Europe. Books on Africa, on the ethnography of savage populations, poets: black poets, and Hikmet, Neruda . . . Eliot, Thomas, Machado, Kavafis . . . Some of the great novelists of the nineteenth century: Dostoyevsky, Gogol . . .

And popularized works of sociology and politics: a history of the Russian revolution. Marx's *Capital,* etc.

The teacher asks — without much hope — if someone would like to act as librarian for the class (and explains what it will entail).

A small young man, Idris, with large teary goat-eyes, the trace of a mustache and beard on his unfledging lips and chin, volunteers. The others, 'Ngomu, Paolino, laugh excitedly, laugh, laugh together, with familiarity for the first time.

12. CLASSROOM SCHOOL KADO. INTERIOR DAY. A FEW DAYS
    LATER.

"If someone has read something, some new books, and wants me to explain something, please ask. It doesn't matter if it takes up some time. Even if it keeps us from going on with our lesson."

No one speaks up. Maybe they have not read anything. They have carried out a silent strike against those unusual books.

Davidson's troubled eyes stare with an obscure trembling. But, finally, he is the one who decides to ask a question.

The teacher's inner voice explodes with joy. It is the first time that a dialogue has taken place.

It is a poor and infantile question:

"What are the cities of Europe like?"

(He has read a novel by . . .)

Such an abyss of inexperience, of inability to conceive of a world for whose culture the teacher is a mediator — to conceive of it in its most simple facts, physical, concrete, practical — strikes him with a sense of terror. But he quickly overcomes it. And, he is overtaken by a chaotic desire.

He begins to talk about a European city: a mixture of Paris, London, Rome, Moscow, with their differences and their similarities becoming entangled: the historical reasons that determine similarities and differences. Churches, palaces, roads, riverside promenades, stadiums, new developments, shanty-towns . . .

13. Classroom School Kado. Interior Day.

It is the first in-class composition.

The teacher dictates the title: "Describe your village." Umpteenth reaction by the students. They are not used to questions that involve them directly, almost physically. They are more used to talking about academic things, things that do not directly concern them. The teacher offers some explanation, some suggestions. Then, tyrannically, he falls back on his authority so as to require them to get to work.

They lower their heads over their paper. And the teacher watches them, he paces and watches over them. (The pink of Africa, outside with its anti-diluvian lines, of mangoes, of mahogany, beyond the clearing of the huts, strangled by the sun.) He watches over them and his inner voice torments him with its continuous, irresolvable problems.

14. Classroom School Kado. Interior Day. The Next Day.

A disaster. The compositions are despicable. Rhetorical thoughts that, having lost the usual outlines, are also grammatically incorrect. This makes them rather humorous. One young man has paraphrased a romantic and rustic poem by a mediocre French poet. As a result, his own village is described with gothic roofs, red brick, beguines, the curate, and even snow!

Davidson did not do the assignment. He handed-in some empty sheets with some uncertain and poor words erased from them.

New indignant scene by the teacher. He cannot keep his anguish and his disappointment to himself. He has them weight heavily on his pupils, a little immaturely like a capricious and frustrated child. He shouts at them, shrill, that they are no longer under the authoritative hand and rhetoric of the colonialists: they are free, free, they are free!

Davidson's troubled eyes stare at him in terror.

15. CLASSROOM SCHOOL KADO. INTERIOR-EXTERIOR DAY. THE NEXT DAY.

Davidson is seated, with his poor dismayed eyes, on his cot in the dormitory.

His mother and father are watching him, with their animal-like nostrils and teeth, from the photo he keeps at the head of the bed. From their woods, from the village square of their town, with the stores, with the laughing children.

He holds his notebooks on his knees. He wants to write. But he does not know what to write, because he does not know what his feelings are, about his village, about the culture that asks him to explain them

He stands. He strolls around the classroom, notebooks in hand. There are the shacks of the high school, empty, the silent courtyards. And down there, with the screams of the animals in the falling night, the forest.

He goes to sit down there near the forest, underneath the funereal monument of a mahogany.

He still tries to give life to emotions that he does not know that he has.

Two or three humble blacks approach: porters, some cook's helpers, who laugh loudly with happiness. They are going to gather wood for their stove. One of them stops along-side of Davidson and they talk. Davidson asks him about his village, which is a distant village in the interior, in Katanka. He answers with wit, simply acting foolish, with his peasantish cheerfulness laughing at the simplicity of his countrymen.

16. Classroom School Kado. Interior Day. The Next Day.

The teacher asks the students to read their compositions out-loud so that the young men can "hear" what they have done through the compelling proof of their readings.

Davidson is first.

He begins to read, with an anguished voice and with troubled eyes that stare up from below. But his composition is quite beautiful . . . Incredible! With peasant joy, with gentle coarseness, with the spirit of a poet — Davidson has written his people, his mother, his brothers, the rites, the superstitions, the dances . . . the hunt for the beasts . . . for lion.

The teachers listens, rapt, word for word, *Image by Image.*

All the poems read will be illustrated by materials from a repertoire relative to the images stimulated by the poems.

16. A, B, C, D, E, F, G, H, I

Interiors and exteriors of Davidson's village and the forest, described by Davidson's voice reading. *(Composition.)*

17. Classroom School Kado. Interior Day.

Davidson is done reading. The teacher is almost in tears. All he can do is tell the young man that he is grateful.

18. Street in Kado. Exterior Day.

The teacher walks through the streets of Kado on a peaceful Sunday. He moves toward the center with the sure and swift step of someone carried by pleasant thoughts.

His inner voice is full of optimism, anxious about the first didactic victory. The future is bright, the feeling of happiness, as on the first day of school, is back: the pink exaltation of Africa.

But wait, there, like in a cubist painting, with the colours of a cubist pallet, Davidson and Idris. They are standing by a crumbling wall — of blinding whiteness — from which hangs a burning purple festoon.

The teacher and students exchange greetings, they begin a conversation first timidly, scared, which then becomes more and more cordial. Together, like young friends, they begin to walk toward the center of the capital. The teacher asks his librarian how the readings are progressing (the students take books out, or keep them there without reading, or read a page a day . . .). He asks Davidson things that are connected to his composition, and so on. When they finally arrive at the center of the city, they have established a mutual confidence and are happy like friends.

More bold discussions, more personal, etc. Love, women, etc.

19. COFFEE-SHOP AT CITY CENTER. INTERIOR DAY.

The teacher offers his students a beer. The discussion, along with being about personal matters, becomes more animated.

Now the young men want to offer their teacher a beer. They invite him to a beer hall that is more familiar to them. It is in what use to be the black quarter. There they talk winking at each other, more than likely a little drunk.

20. AFRICAN BEER PARLOR. EXTERIOR-INTERIOR DAY.

The black quarter: with its colonial homes, the whiteness, the dust, the Indian stores, the sordid interiors of each public place, the colourful landscape, odd, the wooden porches . . .

The beer-parlor, on the second floor of a dirty and fragile building, with an interior courtyard and dance-floors full of drunken or happy blacks going around and around from one room to another.

Everyone enters a private room where the beer is served.

The room that the teacher and his students enter, excited and sweaty, is a large gray empty room that overlooks the street. In the middle of it is a heavy wooden table, with three equally heavy chairs around it. Two cots with gray spreads — terribly gray — along the walls.

They sit down. Every now and then the door opens, someone looks in and then leaves. A young black woman, with a curly short mane of hair like a young man's and wearing a flowered gown, serves the beer.

She laughs joyfully, speaks with the young men in the language of Kado.

Then other waitresses come. They too laugh, laugh. They introduce themselves to the teacher, offering their humble hands of curly headed waitresses.

Faced with so much coarse and candid joy, Davidson cannot but confide in the professor, winking. Of course, the teacher already knew.

He offers the girls a drink, etc.

The laughter becomes more frequent and louder, as does the conversation in African. Until even Davidson and Idris begin to laugh, with their vast shyness, that pools deep within their eyes.

They have to make up their mind to tell their teacher what exactly it is that makes the beer-parlor girls laugh so much. Davidson tells him, interrupted by laughter and truncated by shyness. The crazy young women are curious to know exactly what the white teacher looks like . . . And he laughs, laughs, poor, troubled Davidson . . . The teacher feels that he can and, in a certain sense, must do it. He gets up and cheerfully asks the two or three girls to follow him. He goes out, laughing in Davidson's direction, who is also laughing, laughing, fired up by the beer and grateful happiness.

21. STREET KADO. EXTERIOR DAY.

Again, it's the three of them on the street where they met. Deplorably cheerful due to the beer and the hours spent together in the sordid beer parlor.

The alcohol has melted away modesty and shyness.

Davidson chances a somewhat absurd question, which he might otherwise never have asked. He asks the teacher: "Sir, what is poetry?"

And here a long absurd dialogue between drunks on poetry, walking along the rubble cemeterial road of Kado.

"But you know what it is!" says the teacher.

"No, I don't know!" the young man protests, shaking his curly head.

"Yes, you know!"

"No, I don't know!"

Idris, in concert, laughs. "Yes, you know!"

"No, I don't know!"

"You are African, you are immersed in poetry!"

"No, poetry is a white man's thing."

"Sing a song from your village!"

Davidson sings a song from his village.

But song and dance are tightly enmeshed in his head. While singing, he begins to dance.

A long song, a long dance.

"There, that is poetry!"

"No, no!" says Davidson stubbornly. "This is not poetry."

"Yes, it is poetry."

"No, no, no!"

"It is poetry!"

"No, it is not poetry!"

They are standing by a wall that is blindingly white, and from which hangs a festoon of buganvillas, a fire so red and furious that it blurs into a macabre violet.

22. STREETS AND SQUARES OF KADO. EXTERIOR DAY. ONE
     MONTH LATER.

It is the third anniversary of the liberation of the State.
The capital is in full celebration. Thousands of smiling blacks,
in white fancy dress, in violent pure colours from a "cubist
palette," as one African poet has said — waving flags, greetings, shout along the desolate streets of the capital, white and
flat like during the cholera epidemics, invaded by the fire of
death.

Jeep, American automobiles, etc. Festoons along the
main street, parades with authoritative figures, in frock-
coats, etc. UN troops, etc.

The students from the high school also participate in the
ceremonies. They walk together, along the crowded street,
etc.

The participate in the ceremonies, acclaim the president.

Then they find themselves in the celebrating city, in the
crowd that divides them, etc.

Davidson and two or three friends (among whom is
Idris) find themselves walking along a less crowded street.
A consulate rises with its neo-classical facade, and its hos-
pice-like form, against some macabre gardens, with flutter-
ing flags.

There is the teacher with some other people, talking,
animated and friendly. They are UN soldiers.

Davidson stands there staring, mute and savage, but the
teacher spots him and calls out: Davidson and his friends go
to him.

The UN soldiers are all very young. They are about the
same age as the black students. The sweet European names
of the young men of the UN, and the abrupt and savage ones
of the young men from the school cross during the introduc-
tions. The teacher is friends with one of the soldiers, who

comes from the same European city, in fact from the same town, lost among the fresh fields touched by one of the rivers that flows down from the Alps.

The white young men and the blacks are cautiously timid but cheerful — as one is at their age — about this little event, for the birth of this acquaintance, etc.

The teacher leaves them alone, he goes into the consular building, between the sentinels in full regalia.

The young men go off for a walk on their own.

Davidson and his friends are hungry for news from their new friends: from the blond Piero, with his prize-fighter's face, from the delicate Bill, with the hips of a dancer, from the dark-haired Gianni, who seemed to have walked out of a classical Italian painting, a Correggio.

A warm friendship is born, out of naive questions, out of respect.

Davidson is quickly drawn by an instinctive sympathy for Gianni, the most sensible among them, as well as the most cheerful and lighthearted. But he is quite coarse. He has little education. He is a mechanic. Davidson, on the other hand is full of cultural questions. The result of his having studied, of being at the penultimate year of high school and, above all, those raised in him still with confusion by the new teacher.

22B. GARDENS IN KADO. EXTERIOR DAY.

Strolling aimlessly, as young people do — followed by songs of celebration sung by groups of people here and there throughout the city — they now walk through the gardens of Kado, with the purples and reds of Stanley's time.

Gianni is unable to sustain a conversation with David-son: he knows nothing about literature, knows nothing about Latin . . . He tries to make due, faking it here and there with some concepts.

There, among the plants of Eden, an old gray latrine triumphs. The young men go in. But on the door — rather, on its three doors — the old imprints from colonial days still remain.

Whites, Arabs, Blacks.

However, they all walk into the same section and there, playing around, Gianni invites Bill to talk about literature with him and Davidson, since Bill himself is a bit of an artist.

22C. STREETS FRONTING MISSION AND MISSION ITSELF.
EXTERIOR-INTERIOR DAY.

The singing, the hoarse singing of celebration, in the burning air. The little white mission. The celebratory songs dissolve in front of it, in the savage cadences of the little black children at catechism.

Bill and Davidson are talking about poetry, because this is Davidson's obsession. Bill studies music: his European friends make fun of him because of his love for "symphonies" and "classical music."

They enter the courtyard of the mission, with the sweet sweet naked little black boys. The missionary — a small, jovial peasant, with the face of a child and a devil's beard — greets them laughing and leads them to the mission's dining room.

There they listen to Bach. A sublime movement that, with its sweet potency, seems to erase everything around, the reality of Africa. It sucks it back into the centuries, there where Europe is Christian and supremely civil.

After a while, Gianni is bored and, with the irresistible charm of his simple youth, he distracts the others from the difficult piece they are listening to . . . He talks about jazz, and women, of beautiful women, ah. . .

23. BUILDING KADO. INTERIOR DAY.

A building of lugubrious colonial splendour, with the misery of crumbling cement walls beneath the velvets . . .

The young men, white and black, are there, in the boldness of youth.

A white woman is stripping. (Davidson has never made love with a white woman: but it's not even a problem to him: "How do you get girls?" he asks Gianni, etc.)

The naked white woman: holds the last item of clothing on her outstretched arm.

24. CLASSROOM SCHOOL KADO. INTERIOR DAY.

For the first time, the students — after Davidson's objections — get up the courage to ask the teacher some questions.

There the teacher is everything. There are no libraries, cultural instruments, associations, theaters, cinemas. There is no family life. (Almost everyone's family lives in the interior, in the "brousse.") They have come to understand that the only voice of culture and, to a certain extent, of life, is that of their white teacher.

They ask some rather simple and practical political questions. The anniversary of the Liberation, shaking their emotions, has also moved their confused desire to know. They do not know the meaning of political parties and political struggle. They have childish and uncertain ideas on everything . . .

The teacher — happy, excited — attempts to explain, but words are not enough. He has an idea. He will found an Autonomous scholastic Association, with the right of "self-government" and "auto-criticism."

25. COURTYARD SCHOOL KADO. EXTERIOR DAY.

The teacher arrives, crosses the yard . . . The huts, the mahoganies . . . in the ferociously immobile pink.

The loud "Brother! Brother!"

The teacher's inner voice urges him on with fervent hope.

It is the day of the Association's first meeting.

It is going to take place in the open, like the village's trials . . . at the margins of the wood, under the round shadow of the splendid and infertile cupola of a mahogany.

The elections of a President: the majority, the minority. The decisions (still unconsciously political) concerning the choice of programs, of address, etc.

26. COURTYARD SCHOOL KADO. EXTERIOR DAY.

It is the Association's first ideological session. Composition: the atomic bomb. Bandung. Illiteracy. Debate among the young men, naive, childish, brimming with wrong ideas still, distorted by previous teachers, etc. But already with some realistic intuition, democratic (for example on the participation of women in cultural and social renewal, etc.).

In the heat of discussion, the young men instinctually revert to their own language. The teacher reads his newspaper in the distance, leaving them free to discuss, to be involved — full of hope.

27. COURTYARD SCHOOL KADO. EXTERIOR DAY.

Something serious has happened. The spokesperson for the political party of the opposition in Kado has been arrested. Jailed.

This represents a real trauma for the students. They had a mythical idea of the political struggle, and they had not expected such actions. Having grown up culturally in their previous academic limbo, now they are absorbed by the idealistic and romantic limbo of the new teachings.

Therefore, the second meeting of the students' cultural Association is less well-attended than the first. Only half of the students are present. The others have either gone off on a walk, or they have preferred to play a game of soccer.

Davidson, Idris, and the other more vivacious and interested students, eagerly discuss the political event and condemn the anti-democratic arrest of the opposition politician.

It is like a shadow, a painful omen of their future, over the young men's recently found freedom.

Long shot.

28. CLASSROOM SCHOOL KADO. INTERIOR DAY.

There is a deep silence in the classroom, something resembling pain or defeat.

The teacher stares at his group seriously, saddened, almost offended — in his childish obstination. They stare back from the blackness of their faces, as if from another world.

"We are now almost at the end of the school year, and you have yet to give me something . . . I have opened myself up to you, offered myself, worked like an idiot, I am not saying I have not made mistakes, or that I have not been imprudent, inexperienced . . . But what I expect of you is to talk about those very mistakes . . . I have laid them bare for you, confessed them to the point of losing my dignity . . . etc. And the Association . . . I gave you the opportunity to express yourselves of your own accord . . . without my tyranny . . . affectionate if you like, but tyranny nevertheless . . . and you have done nothing . . . You have been unable to take advantage of your freedom . . ."

Davidson's eyes stare in dismay.

But, while the teacher is talking, it becomes obvious that something odd is happening outside, around the school grounds.

Distant shouting, the roar of jeep motors . . . on the pink exterior of Africa sunken into the sun . . . And some shots.

Curiosity, panic.

Teachers, students, they all leave the classroom. Orders not to go outdoors, screams. The students from the other classes, the other teachers, shaken . . .

The shouting and shooting are getting closer . . .

Then a deep silence, immemorial: the pink of Africa pours into the sun. And then, a group of soldiers running, blacks . . . running away like beasts . . . Some jeeps with other soldiers appear . . . Those running turn around shooting . . . One is hit and falls to the ground, his stomach in the dust.

The others disappear into the forest.

Carousel of jeeps, shooting.

Then silence once more, the pink, the horrendous pink of Africa, in its sun without meaning, pure forgetful fire, that however, now, it has within itself, in its funereal pall that tastes of animal manure, a new presence and so familiar.

A corpse, with its belly in the dust, lost in a secret grieving monologue with himself, with a bit of coagulated blood.

The students gather around that corpse in silence, to stare at it, unable to understand, stupefied by its silence.

The eyes, Davidson's poor sad eyes that stare, beside himself with dismay.

28. A, B, C, D, E. Places Around the African State.
Exterior-Interior. Night and Day.

It is the teacher's inner voice that, *Image by Image,* paints a portrait of that which it calls the "real" African condition (much different from its idealistic and idyllic hopes). The moment is frightening: it is the horrendous epopeia of the Congo that is being evoked.

Mercenary troops that occupy centers in the capital, insulting, arrogant, searching blacks and europeans.

Exodus of blacks.

Concentration camps for black tribes, in a state of horrible poverty.

Young soldiers on drugs.

Agreements between the ex-owners of the colony and black leaders.

Artificially created divisions between tribes, so as to re-create conditions favourable for neo-colonial exploitation.

The disastrous economic situation, the decadence of that little bit which the white colonizers had created in the country. Confusion and chaos in the villages of the forest, in the streets of the city, bare and flat like lazarets, overwhelmed by the warmth of death.

29. CLASSROOM SCHOOL KADO. INTERIOR DAY.

It is time for goodbyes.

The last day of school is like all the other last days of school around the world. A bit of commotion, a bit of joy, the waiting for something that will come, the farewell to something that has ended. Saying good-bye to his students, the teacher takes a calmer, though still bitter, exam of the common experience of that first year: poor results, but better than nothing. But, then, would European students have been any better? Equally absent, of course, but maybe even capable of irony and vulgarity toward the idealistic teacher.

"The moment has arrived for us to say good-bye in the midst of a difficult moment for your nation. But, no matter how humiliating, sad or tragic that it may be, always remember that you are free men."

30. SCHOOL IN KADO. INTERIOR-EXTERIOR DAY.

Davidson prepares his small bag, seated on the cot in his dormitory. He gathers, with religious respect, his humble wardrobe, the books, the photos. This is the basic equipment of many students around the world, all the same, with their problems, their humiliations, the nobility of their future, as yet un-tainted. He steps out with his bundle.

Some of his other "intern" friends are also ready.

Many have already left, the school — the barracks of the classrooms, the courtyards — is almost all empty.

A column of jeeps and trucks is ready in the clearing between the moth-eaten huts and mahoganies in front of the school.

They are UN vehicles, and they are moving toward the interior.

They will accompany the young men toward their villages for a ways at least.

Gianni is there, in his jeep, with the cheerful smile of a young European industrial labourer; and Piero, and Bill.

Davidson gets in to ride with them.

The teacher is in front of the school watching the departure — lovingly, like a brother, and a little tense from emotion.

The column departs — the last good-byes sound from the jeeps.

And the school becomes distant.

Another gesture, a dumbfounded smile from Davidson.

And the school grows more distant.

"Good-bye, Davidson, now you are alone. You are going back to your Africa alone . . . like to a dying mother. Son of its mystery that is nothing more than the terror of prehistory, go toward your mystery, with a humble baggage of acquaintances . . . Alone, to measure that disproportion that is vast like the continents and infinite like the millennia . . . in that pink of death, alone, now, alone . . .

The school is now distant, a few scattered and lost barracks against an atrociously pink expanse.

31. A, B, C, D, E, F, G. PLACES AROUND THE AFRICAN STATE. INTERIORS-EXTERIORS.

Image by Image, evoked by the teacher's inner voice, the internal situation of the State appears still charged, to the point of tragedy. Divided by tribal infighting, it is contested by neo-colonial capital.

— Slaughter of whites in a village.

— Fighting in the forest.

— State of anarchy in the capital, with summary executions.

— Torture of Africans, atrocious humiliation of whites.

— Uprisings within the concentration camps — full of hungry black beasts — that develop into new massacres.

32. FOREST VILLAGE DAVIDSON. EXTERIOR DAY.

The jeep column arrives, through the forest — a path of reddish earth — among celestial greens, poisoned greens, tangled into capricious layers, in a splendid and sterile display — at the edges of a desolate town, a large square surrounded by wooden homes, with porches, and the white storehouses.

Davidson gets out of the jeep, bids his friends good-bye and, with his bundle, takes the path toward his village, a few miles from the deserted town. It is as if the plague had broken out and made of the everyday peace a peace without tomorrow.

33. FOREST SCORCHED BY SUNLIGHT. EXTERIOR DAY.

Davidson walks, alone, quickly, along the reddish path, toward his village.

Suddenly, for no particular reason, he becomes aware of something: he sees, for the first time, the forest of his native village, which he had certainly seen many times in his youth.

It is a discovery for him (maybe guided by the awareness that he acquired through his poetic composition at school) and he stops to stare ahead, enchanted. It is but a common scene from the African interior: with its pink background, over which the capricious and funereal profiles of the equatorial trees imbricate themselves. And the sounds, the bestial voices. The prehuman anxiety that reigns there, with its deathly peace.

34. 35. 36. DAVIDSON'S ARRIVAL AT THE VILLAGE.

Meeting with his relatives, father, mother, brothers, greetings according to ancient tradition, dances, interminable nocturnal dance, obsessive, passionate, etc.

37. POLITICAL ARGUMENT BETWEEN DAVIDSON AND HIS
    FATHER.

As a tribal chief, his father takes the side of the African chiefs, who are in agreement with the large neo-colonial mineral companies. He is readying to fight against a tribe that is a traditional enemy and faithful to the central government.

38. DANCES AND RITUALS IN PREPARATION FOR WAR.

Davidson becomes embroiled, involved. His knowledge of the real political situation, of the real economic interests, of the real archaic nature of tribal hate that is involved in the contemporary conflict, is too weak.

39. CLASH BETWEEN TRIBES.

Davidson's father's tribe sacks and commits atrocities in the enemy village. It is left in the funereal light of the sun, a pile of burned huts, of corpses strewn over the blinding dust.

40. FOREST. EXTERIOR DAY.

Intervention by UN troops.

The group that has Gianni, Piero and Bill runs through the forest, toward the region that is the center of the African battles and European interests. It is a platoon of young soldiers. They kid around, laugh, they have the heavy and vulgar spirit of the barracks: and in the moment of the fight, their language is tainted with traces of racism, with a hate for people of colour.

41. FOREST AND VILLAGE DAVIDSON. EXTERIOR DAY.

The spirituality of the savage soldiers in some corner of the forest in stark contrast with the practical and vulgar prosaicness of the UN soldiers.

The former carry out an absurd rite — a dance for victory, or atonement to the gods for future battles: and, in the obsession of that religious act, in the mad exaltation of the archaic soul, the dark and powerful forces of the spirit dominate.

Davidson becomes more and more involved, even though he participates from the margins, like a European, like a foreigner.

42. FOREST. EXTERIOR DAY.

The racing jeeps.

There is calm among the young soldiers: they gradually leave behind the places that have been, for better or for worse, under white control for a long time — maybe it is an unconscious fear that halts their play and their laughter. They have stopped kidding one another as military ritual and the rhetoric of their conformist world require, and they talk to each other more humanely. They tell their individual stories, the story of their life: they become human.

43. FOREST VILLAGE DAVIDSON. EXTERIOR DAY.

More and more inhuman is the fanatic exaltation of the Africans. Now a meeting takes place in the space in which the hut villages of Davidson's tribe are organized — a lugubriously European space, with small brick constructions, a mission with its church.

An Africa chief, dressed as for ceremony with a brimmed hat, like a European dandy, is making an insane speech to the inhabitants of the village who listen in a state of excitement.

44. FOREST AND TOWN. EXTERIOR AT DUSK.

The UN soldiers in their jeep continue to race through the forest. The sun is setting, a bloody colour invades the immemorial reign of the beasts.

A woad fills with shadow.

The platoon arrives at the margins of a town — let's call it Kindu: the usual houses of the plague-ridden, the fragile colonial constructions, the silence.

The jeeps are put in place, the tents are pitched in silence: the dialogues become less and less vulgar, in the quiet of practical work in the falling night.

In the nearby town, there is a frightening peace. Some blacks come to buy or sell things. There is some laughter in the air, a playful voice here and there. Some whites also arrive, with bad news. They drink with their compatriots, according to the conformism of colonial rituals, the old rhetoric of action and national glory.

45. FOREST VILLAGE DAVIDSON. EXTERIOR NIGHT.

The talking stops with the falling shadows. The last ritual begins. The young drug themselves, etc.

Like an obedient son, Davidson partakes in that which the other young men of the tribe do. In his gentle but sad eyes, an immemorial drunkenness trembles, a terrible light.

46. TOWN (UN CAMP). EXTERIOR NIGHT.

Kindu is finally immersed in silence: in the curfews before the deluge. Only in the UN Camp there are signs of life.

The young men in their tents get ready for bed. They are washing themselves and their clothing. Others talk as they wait for sleep to overtake them.

Bill puts on one of his records, the one he loves the most: a sublime piece by Bach.

His friends kid him about it a little, but discreetly now, almost timidly. And Bill shows that there is nothing to make fun of because one can dance even to that rigorous rhythm of pure music. In fact, he does so. He dances happily like a child.

Gianni is seated near his tent, with his Correggio face reclining on his shoulder.

That great music of Europe, his Europe, recalls — against his will (it is time for nostalgia) — for him his town, his countryside. He says so outloud, to the others — kidding, of course. But then he really loses himself in his fantasy, memory by memory, *Image by Image.*

46. A, B, C, D, E, F, G. EUROPEAN LOCALES EVOKED BY THE
    MUSIC. EXTERIOR-INTERIOR DAY.

— Pan across an almost abandoned large villa from the 1700s with rows of delicate white columns, and large awkward deteriorating putti. . . A large and harmonious construction, on a green field of secular grass that now dominates the old magnificence with rustic humility.

— Pan across the cellars and stores of the sharecroppers organized in the wings of the old villa, with the abandoned tools, in silence, in the humid sun-drenched grass.

— Pan across a peasants' cottage nearby, with the stone walls blue from sulfate — the Sunday silence on the threshing floor — and distant bells. Pan across the beams, the carts, the coulter blades abandoned on the mould.

— Pan across Gianni, straddling his bicycle in his Sunday best, a flower at his lapel.

— Pan across to the girl that he is looking at down there, on the edge of the white road, against a background of tender jasmine, of vines — she is talking with other girls, all young, with thick hair, like peasant women, in their best red or green dresses.

— Greetings exchanged between Gianni and the girl . . . and . . .

— The little square in front of the church, as it empties after mass, to the louder sound of the bells, over the cobblestones of the town, dark and white to the blinding mid-day sun of spring.

— And the friends that pass by, elegant and ironic, with their great barbarian curls, bicycles in tow . . . laugh at Gianni, still lost in his gaze of the girl of his heart . . . who leaves, composed and proper, among her girlfriends who succeed in tearing a tormented and timid smile from her every now and then.

— Young boys who run by with their new games, causing a commotion in the almost empty square, in the sonorous silence of the hour of the mid-day meal.

— Gianni is now alone, riding his bicycle along the white road between the fields abandoned to the silence, with a hint of something pure, something religious. The sun extends a peace that nothing could ever disturb, ever. . . among the long rows of vineyards, and jasmines and, down beyond, the silver formations of poplars.

But something horrible, now, cuts through that peace, cuts through Bach's music that evokes it, fatally . . . something horrible, a frightening violence: shots, bursts of gunfire, and shouts — the shouts of men in anger, shouts of dying men. Shots, bursts of gunfire. A deafening laceration that takes away one's breath and.

47. Town (UN Camp). Exterior Night.

Gianni is on the ground, bleeding. The camp has been destroyed. The bodies of the others are strewn around. In the shadows of the forest, in the open spaces of the town, the last shots, the last shouts.

48. Town (UN Camp). Exterior Day.

It is now day. The light floods Gianni's body — with the absent fire of its useless violence — and around him, desecrated, torn from the magic darkness of night, to be offered to an even more tremendous piety — that of the sun — the forest, the town, with its open spaces, its modest buildings white like hospices, and the red dust: in the silence of millennia.

49. Town. Exterior Day.

Who knows who might have dragged Gianni's body elsewhere. On a street at the center of the small colonial city . . . with white stairways . . . maybe a consulate . . . and a garden in complete neglect . . . a well . . .

Gianni is there now, arms outstretched: and nearby - with him and a bit of coagulated blood — another dead man meditates.

A deep, burning silence, and then . . . some people walk by in the distance, turn the corner of another street . . . the voices disappear.

Then a young black man passes by, almost running. He holds a bundle tight under his arm and, running, turns to an invisible interlocutor or witness on the other side of the street, and laughs in his direction, shouting mysterious words, of agreement? of provocation? He runs off.

Two other young black men, behind him. They too run, joyful like school-children who might have played a trick on someone, and go off laughing and talking excitedly between themselves.

50. Forest Near Town. Exterior Day.

The same mysterious hands, or other hands, have taken Gianni's body into the forest, into an atrociously pink clearing, with its circle of mangoes and mahoganies lost in the useless beauty of their design.

Women pass quickly by the body — now face up — with little black children at their skirts — coloured skirts, of cotton, patterned with suns and peacocks.

The eldest, she too holds in her arms a bundle in silence, an absurd and sordid bundle.

Another body beside Gianni's, in that atrocious pink clearing, has been mutilated, is missing an arm.

51. SUN-DRENCHED FOREST. EXTERIOR DAY.

Gianni is now in the same clearing through which Davidson had passed on his way to his village, and which he had "recognized" as if in a vision.

Now Gianni's body has also been mutilated.

52. FOREST AND VILLAGE DAVIDSON. EXTERIOR NIGHT.

Davidson's father, his mother, his brothers, his friends from the village — drugged, made insane by the bloody exaltation, by the terror, by the archaic spirituality that possesses them — undertake with the complicity of night, around raging fires . . . a complex ritual, who knows who invented it, to whom it may be dedicated, for what mysterious connections of thought and for what reasons: as if natural, elemental. An old ritual of the tribe in prehistory.

53. ROAD SCHOOL KADO. EXTERIOR DAY.

Discouraged, excited, the teacher comes forward through the opening among the huts, mahoganies, etc. in the "atrociously pink clearing." It is the first day of school of the new year.

He walks slowly, perspiring. The impulse that had dragged him toward school during the previous year, and which had enchanted him with the voices of the students at play calling "Brother! Brother!" to each other, seems to have abandoned him. He is there only because of heroic determination; maybe fully aware of the uselessness of his duty.

The students are there playing. He, with an affectionate gaze, looks over at them but does not stop: he goes directly toward the long barracks of the school, and enters.

54. Classroom School Kado. Interior Day.

The classroom, the seat of so many useless idealistic battles. What has happened in between, between the full classroom of the previous year and this empty classroom, brimming with useless waiting! The historic delusion of a new democracy, the failure of freedom, regression, the reaction of the European bourgeoisie, everything reverberates down there, in the land of forests, through the underhanded byways of corruption, of ignorance.

Then the students who walk in and look over the teacher who waits for them — incomprehensible with their eternal sweetness.

They enter in silence and sit at their desks: here they are seated all in a row, 'Ngomu, Paolino, Idris, Davidson . . . They do not dare speak, merely look.

A deep embarrassment divides the teacher from his students: it seems impossible that the silence might be broken.

But what deep affection, in those incomprehensible stares . . . What expectation . . . what a grateful desire . . .

Idris — it is a miracle — stands up — with his sweet goatish head, and the large shining eyes — and, as if possessed by a sentiment anterior to himself, runs up to shake the teacher's hand . . . And further, since the teacher — stupefied and happy — has a bit of affection for him — he embraces him, like one might embrace a father, a brother.

Then, the other students, overtaken by a similar sentiment, stand and run toward the teacher's desk. They gather tightly around the teacher, touching his hand, embracing him.

It is like the meeting of old friends, who only after meeting each other after a long time become aware of the real affection that had bound them to each other previously, of the importance that it may have had in their life.

Everyone happily goes to greet their teacher. Only Davidson, who had stood up along with the others, sits aside on his own with a terrible shadow in the eyes that appear to be blind.

55. CLASSROOM SCHOOL KADO. INTERIOR DAY.
THE FOLLOWING DAY.

A storm of questions.

During their holidays the students either read the teacher's books, or the readings from the previous year have matured within them.

A tempest of questions:

"Sir, what does commitment mean?"

"Sir, who is the better poet? Eliot, who was a Christian, or Esenin, who was Soviet?"

"Sir, could you tell us the real meaning of the word neo-colonialism?"

"What is the Mining Society?"

"Are there the remnants of primitive States, of archaic and prehistoric societies in Europe?"

"And what is the subproletariat? Are colonized peoples subproletarian? Are Algerians subproletarians? And what is the meaning of the war for independence and the revolution for subproletarians?"

" Is nationalism a serious problem for us?"

" Who were Hitler and Mussolini?"

" Does Fascism still exist in Europe?"

A tempest of questions.

And it is one long, dramatic, happy, how can one describe it?, press conference, in which the teacher, overtaken by the impatience and insatiable curiosity of the students, does not tire of the questions, making their problems clear to himself and to them, naive or mature, infantile or adult.

The only one who does not take part in the discussion
— but seems nevertheless to be listening, or maybe not even,
as he sits there closed in a craving, ill silence — is Davidson.

56. COURTYARD SCHOOL KADO. EXTERIOR DAY.

Beneath the great umbrella of the mahogany, gathered
in a circle like the council of some ancient peoples, the young
men of the high school are busy with a meeting of their
"Association." They discuss — as they had never done before
— the issues addressed the day before. In their own language, what is now the official language of the Association.

As usual, a little in dispart, as a simple "observer," is the
teacher, smoking and reading his paper.

Davidson is silent. He is there like a child among grown-
ups. Paralyzed by a restless inability to express himself,
maybe wanting to, maybe humble — he just listens, trying
hard to participate. But what keeps him outside of all this,
distant, somber, angry in exclusion, is like a disease.

This time the teacher watches him. He watches him for
quite a while, understands the pain. He becomes aware of a
new problem that he might be facing, and which will inter-
rupt the course of the great satisfaction he is feeling as a
teacher, etc.

He gets up and approaches Davidson, forces him to get
up and begins to ask him some questions — what is it, how
do you feel, I don't recognize you any more . . .

Useless questions that fall into the desperate silence of
the young man.

The teacher takes him by the arm, drags him along and
talks to him, talks, questions. Useless. Then he stands in
front of him, staring into his eyes, shaking him by the
shoulders . . .

Davidson stares back too, into his eyes but — in reverse shot, in front of him — he does not see the teacher's face but. . .

. . . The landscape of the "sun-drenched forest," that which had appeared to him as a vision, on his way back home.

Now it is there, in front of his eyes, immovable, in a still frame, without sound, without voices, without a breath of air.

The teacher's voice, anguished, resounds outside of the camp — upon that silence of funereal mahoganies, mangoes, sycamores capriciously scattered within the pink clearing, a landscape of beasts thirsty for blood.

Then slowly the teacher's voice also vanishes.

All that is left in front of Davidson's eyes is, mute and terrible, the vision of the forest.

57. CLASSROOM SCHOOL KADO. INTERIOR DAY.

Davidson is at his desk, present and distant. He stares with the sad eyes of a ferocious and bewildered black man.

The teacher keeps an eye on him throughout the lesson — he is overtaken by tremendous sympathy. He does not yet know the reasons for that illness: he feels only pity. He knows that he has to intervene upon Davidson's illness, heal him, return him to reality from the obscurity of his nightmare.

He looks at Davidson with compassion, but he knows nothing. The first method is to try and shake him, furiously, with a violent jolt . . .

He interrupts the lesson and asks Davidson to repeat that which he has just explained. Davidson looks back lost, pleading, but does not utter a word.

The teacher pretends to get angry, with a violence that had never before been displayed in that classroom.

Davidson looks at him terrified. The terror spreads its colour through the faces of his classmates like a disease.

58. CLASSROOM SCHOOL KADO. INTERIOR DAY.

The teacher punishes Davidson by having him write a summary of all of the last series of literature lessons.

Davidson comes to class — always automatic, absent, like a child among adults: and the teacher asks him to read what he has written.

Davidson has tried to do as told, diligently, and he begins to read. But his work is childishly scholastic, painful, something which in reality, in another sort of school — that of all the preceding years — was quite acceptable. The teacher listens with pity, hoping to understand what has happened to the young man.

Suddenly, Davidson interrupts himself — and his sad eyes, cut by a sweet and evil light, gaze into the void.

In front of him is the absolute forest. Mute, immobile, irrevocable.

The teacher, overtaken by an impulsive, impotent rage, stands up and, exasperated, assails him verbally.

Davidson, shaking his hands in front of his eyes, as if to erase that which he sees, is able to eradicate himself from his vision. He is able to hear the voice of the teacher who overwhelms him, interrogates him, and calls to him.

He begins to scream. It is a terrible scream, like a wounded beast. He stands and then falls to the ground, among the desks, rolling, screaming and screaming.

59. STREETS KADO OR SCHOOL COURTYARD KADO. EXTERIOR DAY.

"You have to help me. I need to know what is happening to Davidson, you are a friend; maybe he'll talk to you."

But Idris shakes his head: "No, sir; I know as much as you do about it . . . My village is in a wholly different part of the region . . . There are more than a thousand kilometers between our villages . . . I am a Muslim, and Davidson is pagan . . . I know nothing, I know nothing."

A pagan young man, a pagan young man, who is a member of Davidson's tribe. 'Ngomu . . . the teacher interrogates 'Ngomu. But Davidson speaks with no one, he spends his time alone. It involves magic . . . Ah, 'Ngomu; poor, lost, pagan, it is not magic, it is a disease that men know well but do not know its causes . . . Davidson is obsessed, but not with spirits; by his conscience, by his soul. But why, what has happened to him over the last few months.

Yes, 'Ngomu is pagan, and his tribe is not far from Davidson's. But over the last few months some terrible, chaotic things have happened; and he knows nothing of what went on in the province where his friend's village is located.

60. ROAD KADO. EXTERIOR DAY.

The blinding white wall, with its purple festoon of glorious, cadaverous bougainvillea.

The teacher walks, engaged by his inner voice: the unimaginable African situations, the soul torn between history and prehistory, solitude, impotence, sweetness . . .

He arrives in front of the Mission.

Beyond the enclosure wall: the Father is there, with his white bell-shaped smock over his large peasant's feet, the sweetest Venetian child's eyes over his mephistophelian beard.

There is a mission at Kindu. Something will turn up about what happened to Davidson, his father, his tribe, Kindu . . .

They walk, with the young black children filing behind them, singing, singing the *Kirie leison* as if it where one of their own old savage dirges. The Father listens, it is certain that he will do his best to help the teacher.

Certainly, some awful things must have happened at the Kindu station. The newspaper in the capital has not covered it. But certainly the European papers have. In the meantime, we will have to try to read those. . .

61. SUN-DRENCHED FOREST. EXTERIOR DAY.

The sun-drenched forest — without a movement, without a voice.

62. RESIDENCE HALL SCHOOL KADO. INTERIOR DAY.

The photograph of Davidson's parents and brothers among their huts — and wide-angle, down, upon Davidson stretched out on his cot.

His eyes are fixed upon the "compulsory image," the forest mute and immobile in the sun.

He stirs so as not to see, he tries to rip that horrendous and most pure of landscapes from his eyes, and moans.

63. COURTYARD SCHOOL KADO. EXTERIOR DAY.

The teacher, walking head-on, among the faint shouts of break-time games, etc.

He holds a letter and a newspaper that he glances at mechanically, as if fascinated by the monstrous thing that is written there in large letters.

He is not reading, he has already read it.

His inner voice drags him, involved, merciless, etc.

"What should I do, there is such a discrepancy between that which has happened and what I can say. I have to tell the truth, the truth, he must hear it, he has to, he has to be confronted by all of it, in all its atrocity, he must no longer ignore it, he must tell himself so, or else he will remain trapped within this rejected terror for the rest of his life. . . poor Davidson, dear boy . . .

64. DORMITORY SCHOOL KADO. INTERIOR DAY.

Davidson is laying there, quiet on his cot, staring into emptiness.

Other young men, Idris, are dispersed around, concentrating on their homework, diligent and silent.

"Davidson, I know what happened this summer in your village . . . I want to tell you this, even if you don't want me to . . . I am not saying that I sympathize with what happened . . . I am not like the fathers of the missions, even if I seem to be, and if I am a little crazy like them! etc.

"I think I understand, or at least I have an historical understanding . . . We have spoken of this so many times in class, you should know what I am talking about . . . I have told you so many times, only through history can we explain that which came before it, what is outside of it, as much as it is part of us . . .

"Then, prehistory will have its revenge, it will humiliate us with its terrible and triumphant incomprehensibility . . . But what can we do? etc.

"I know everything, those few simple things that you do not want to know. But only reason can save you, and reason rejects sentimentalism, mysteries, pain . . . Reason is whole, it is sound . . .

"Listen to me, Davidson . . . and forgive me . . ."

"You, in your village, with your father and brothers, betrayed yourself; the one real Davidson in Africa and on this earth! Forgive me if I make light of it . . . But, well, at least . . . you have forgotten to act like a modern and civil man . . . Oh, no, not of your own fault . . . You were transported back into the centuries, you gave in. You drugged yourself, you participated in rituals that are no longer yours, and as such are guilty in themselves.

You have killed, tortured; you participated in the massacre of your friends, the young men of the UN! With your village, you participated in a ritual . . ."

Davidson gets up from his cot and lunges for his small suitcase. There he takes out a large knife, and shouting that it's not true, it's not true, he throws himself at the teacher. They fall to the ground, the hand with the knife rises, and falls . . .

Idris and the others run, they tear Davidson away from the teacher etc. The teacher is bleeding. Davidson runs from the dormitory screaming like an animal, and is swallowed by the sunlight that beats upon the dreadful clearing.

65. STREETS AND GARDENS OF KADO. EXTERIOR DAY.

Davidson runs like a screaming beast through the city.

The wall with its boungavillas.

The mission with the voices of the young men singing the *Kirie leison*.

The streets of what was once the black quarter.

And burning in front of Davidson's eyes . . .

. . . the haunting and insuppressible vision, of the sun-drenched forest.

He arrives in the gardens, the useless, macabre earthly paradise, with its festoons of bougainvilias, and thousands of flowers gathered in the peace of a summer without end.

He falls into a flower bed wailing. Looks up. An animal. Another ferocious animal on the grass, their monstrous life, their hunger, their motivation lost in the recesses of pure existence.

He gets up, his eyes lost in the void, he wanders along the empty gardens.

At the latrine from colonial times: the section for whites, the section for arabs, the section for blacks.

Out of an impulse that is born in the recesses of the soul, he walks in, degraded, mechanically, into the section for blacks, in the sun's buzzing penumbra.

Davidson is in front of the horrible wall of the latrine. And his terrified eyes stare. But in a reverse shot, in front of himself, he does not see the wall, but . . .

. . . relentless, the form of the forest, the sun.

With what is by now a mechanical impulse — of an animal that moves its fins or small paws in front of its eyes — he tries to tear that vision from his eyes, but he cannot.

The vision of the forest, sweet, is there in front of him.

Then, suddenly, pronounced only by his inner voice, a word resounds.

66. SUN-DRENCHED FOREST. EXTERIOR DAY.

It is the first word of a poem. With that word something begins to stir in the forest.

A weak breath of wind that flows among the funereally elegant leaves of the mahoganies and mangoes.

Another word: and the voices can be heard, the sounds of the forest, its monstrous breath and its daily croaking of birds, splashes, sighs.

A third word . . .

A long panning shot, to discover the life that nests in the forest in deathly peace. A bird flies, questioning, innocent.

Women pass by, with their children on their back, with their cheerful eyes.

There is no conclusion to the poem, it stops in the forest, lost in its sad and magnificent sun — alive.

67. CLASSROOM SCHOOL KADO. INTERIOR DAY.

Silence. The silence of one of the many school days. The
young men are writing an in-class composition. The teacher
watches them etc. Silence, sun.

As the young men gradually finish, they hand-in their
assignment and leave the room.

Davidson has finished writing, with the slow, ambiguous, and mechanical gestures of a sick person.

He stands up, furtive, uncertain. He leaves his composition on the teacher's desk, glancing into the teacher's
watchful eyes . . . Then, as if frightened, as if he had done
something wrong, he runs off.

The teacher looks at the paper with uncontrollable anxiety — it's a poem.

The poem that was spoken to Davidson on the previous
day by his own inner voice.

(At this point there will be a sweet explosion of music
by Bach.)

68. COURTYARD SCHOOL KADO. EXTERIOR DAY.

Holding the sheet of paper on which the poem is written, the teacher leaves the classroom and runs off to look for
Davidson.

His inner voice exults:

"It is beautiful, beautiful, I will tell him that it is so
beautiful, that it is a poem, and poor Davidson, poor poet,
what a price he had to pay to become one! . . . I will have it
published for him, yes, in a European journal . . . it is beautiful
Davidson, it is beautiful . . ."

69. DORMITORY SCHOOL KADO. INTERIOR DAY.

Crouched on his cot, with a satchel on his knees, Davidson is writing again. He is so intent at his task, his sweet

curly-haired head bent over the papers, with his sad eyes lost in dream, that he is not aware of being watched.

The words of the new poem are again being dictated by the inner voice in its familiar timbre. Word for word, image by image, in the sweet and severe wave of the Bach sonata, here is his poem.

70. A, B, C, D, E, F, G, H, I. AFRICAN LANDSCAPES POEM. EXTERIOR DAY.

It will not be a joyous poem, or one of "pure life." Rather, it will be of pain, delusion, and a critique, yes, that's it, a critique. A harsh sentiment of rational passion — even if still a little timid — on the sweet sentiment of the living things of Africa.

— What will be shown are little children, with their lively yet adult eyes, and their mothers, in Kindu.

— The great squares of red dust, surrounded by the flat city of hospices, colonial buildings, and abandoned gardens.

— The ceremonies of an emerging civil life.

The horror of the massacres. (Poem.)

71. DORMITORY SCHOOL KADO. INTERIOR DAY.

Only when he has finished writing does Davidson become aware of the presence of his teacher.

He stands, confused, desperate, respectful. They stare at each other.

A troubled and innocent smile — as a greeting, as a justification, as a way of being — breaks its light upon Davidson's face.

THE END

APPENDIX

The trial for my film La Ricotta, for disparagement of the church,
kept me from filming *The Savage Father*. The pain this caused me
— and which I have attempted to express in these naive verses
of "And Africa?" — still burns inside of me. I dedicate this script
of *The Savage Father* to the State Prosecutor and the Judge who
indicted me.

AND AFRICA?

The red and yellow face, nuanced
in the baldness on top, in the smooth
round chin below: its little mustache,
red and cruel in profile, like that of
a middle-aged Lanzichenecco down from Terre,
with its spired roofs and frozen rivers. . .
This face, that stared at me
with its blue but classic eyes,
from behind a rustic table,
one for grand beaurocrats,
while outside atomic bombs exploded
in the yellowish evening sky of twenty years ago.
Then he started — swollen
with hysterics, and red
like a bloody foreskin —
to admonish me, to call me crazy . . .
And I . . . innocent, offended . . . listened,
tears and protest swirling uselessly
in my throat of adolescent
still dressed by his mother: He,
a practical man, was right:
I had spent too much money on useless refineries,
and I had also touched the sensitivity of the great,
they too innocent in their glorious private lives.
I listened. He did not explode, yet:

even his Lanzichenecco throat was that of a boy,
nevertheless, deaf tears were mixing at the lecture.
The pout beneath the red mustache, yellowish,
was the sign of something sacred
that was taking place in his breast.
And I: "I did not know, how could I have known,
I have been doing this work for only a year!"
And more confused, angry words I cannot remember.
Meanwhile, his face seemed to cleave in two:
or, rather, for an instant, he appeared to be
someone else who, leaning over a threshold,
not too far from the table, in the light
of that ancient evening of a yellowed war.
He was the one who was really in charge and,
in fact, he said to the squire (momentarily silenced):
"What does an extra expense matter,
now that I have stopped all production!"
And I felt a little relieved.
But the other, there, who through osmosis
had emerged from Bini's thorax, was my father.
The unmentioned father, unremembered
since December of fifty-nine, when he died.
Now he was there, almost benevolently in charge:
my coetaneous from Gorizia, then he was once more
red-haired, hands in his pockets,
heavy like a parachutist after mess-hall.
Resolved, like this, to my partial advantage
the question of the other film
— dreamed a little earlier and persistent
with rural and desert images in the new dream —
there was a brief silence, apparently heavy
with consolation, but actually of clear pain.
I stepped closer to him, who meanwhile
was leaning against a wall in the room
behind me, gathered in silence,
I stepped closer, and timidly almost on his face . . .
afterall it was only my father's face,
with its gray skin of drink and death,
I whispered: "And . . . Africa?

And the flamboyants of Mombasa?
The red branches, against the green leaves,
red stylistic sample on a green background,
red and green
without which my soul could no longer live?"
Ah, father no longer mine now, father nothing more
than father, who come and go in my dreams,
when you wish,
like a boar on a hook, gray with wine and death
coming forward to say terrible things,
to reestablish old truths,
with the pleasure of someone who has tried them,
dying in the cheap old matrimonial bed,
vomiting blood from your innards onto the sheets,
traveling for one day and one night
in a casket toward the inhospitable Friuli
on a sunny winter's day of nineteenfiftynine!
The world is the reality that you have always
         paternally wanted.
And I, son who systematically tried everything,
every tormented thing that sons must try,
I find myself here again, first guinea-pig
         for an unknown pain,
to prefigure the case of the impossibility
"to express one's self due to greater forces";
thing that no poet, severe owner of a humble pen,
ever had to fear through the centuries.
Martyrdom, a little ridiculous like all martyrdoms.
But in the great paternal normality of dreams
and life afterall, how moving,
is my wish to die, in the dream,
for the disappointing loss of that red and green!

January 30, 1963

COLONIALISM AS A "STRUCTURE THAT WANTS TO BE ANOTHER STRUCTURE"

Pier Paolo Pasolini, writer, film-maker and essayist, made his debut in 1948, with a small volume of poems written in his mother's Friulian language. This act of writing in the language of a subculture was the first instance in what would be the author's life-long engagement and interest in subaltern cultures. In the late 1940s, as a teacher and active member of the Italian Communist Party (PCI) in the Friuli (then an impoverished area of Northeastern Italy), Pasolini began to suffer the animosity of normative forces of the time. His pedagogical and organizational activities among workers and peasants pressed a local priest to take action against Pasolini. He was denounced as a homosexual threat to his young male pupils, an accusation that resulted not only in Pasolini's being relieved of his teaching post, but also in his expulsion from the PCI in 1949. That series of events brought into greater focus the apparently contradictory dimensions of Pasolini's life: homosexuality, Marxism, and Catholicism represent a crucially active set of circumstances that colored Pasolini's art and his relationship with Italian society until his assassination/murder in 1975.

From 1949 to 1977, two years after his murder, Pier Paolo Pasolini was the subject of approximately thirty-three trials on a variety of charges: "offensiveness toward good customs and to the common sense of morality and decency" (for *Mamma Roma*, 1962); "contempt toward the state religion, under the pretext of cinematographic description, by mocking the figure and value of Christ through musical commentary, mimicry, dialogue" (for *La Ricotta*, 1963); representation of "scenes offensive to the public decency in the depiction of intercourse between the guest and the maid, the woman of the house, and with the male components of the household, as well as the homosexual tendencies of the head of the household, the father, which are contrary to every moral value, social and familial" (for *Teorema*, 1968); calls of "blasphemous, subversive, pornographic, indecent" (for *The Decameron*, 1971); charges of "a film full of obscenities . . . nothing more than a series of vulgar exhibitions of sexual organs, all very clearly photographed" (for *Arabian Nights*, 1973).

While all the charges are aimed at what may be most obviously offensive to a conservative sector of the population, they hide a more insidious challenge to cultural and ideological diversity behind catch-phrases such as "common decency" and "public morality." What is achingly apparent in any of Pasolini films is that the author does not merely seek to shock but aims to present a worldview that is ideologically conflictual to, and compromising for, the dominant culture.

Pasolini proposed and produced art "as an exploration of the unsaid in common and official ideological discourses." The effectiveness of his art lies in his portrayal of "something that scandalizes for its being what it is. It scandalizes because of its nature: because for one reason or another it is a diverse nature" (Ferrero, 2). "Diverse" is my translation of *diverso*, which would also literally translate to "different," and this term would become for Pasolini representative of a concept central to his life and work. Used in Italian as a colloquialism in reference to homosexuality, Pasolini set himself the task of diffusing the term of its negative connotations by infusing it with a sense of cultural importance and militancy. Largely biographical at its inception, the concept acquired cultural and political dimensions by which the author sought to bridge various manifestations of the diverse (homosexuality, sub-proletarianism, Third World cultures) in a common oppositional front against officialdom.

According to Pasolini, people's physicality, their bodies and sexual organs, identify them as peripheral products of specific socio-economic conditions and a-historic conditions. Therefore, since "the language of action or simply of offensive presence [is a] stage of pre-revolutionary contestation," official culture finds it necessary to silence or censor these bodies and render them invisible. The uninhibited display of sub-proletarian bodies one witnesses in most of Pasolini's films is offensive to societal norms because it offers a code of being that demystifies the ideal body of bourgeois representation and proposes (sub)alternatives to it. Aside from a sign of potentially revolutionary value, the "language of action" represented by those bodies is also representative of a diversity of spoken language, the dialects, which, as an infraction of accepted cultural codes, signals a non-negotiable threat contained within the potentiality of subaltern self-expression.

Pasolini, himself a diverse and bourgeois intellectual, becomes aware of his own need to give up the standardized language of Italian intellectual culture and become initiated into a revolutionary one. His is double initiation: first into the language of Marxism, and then into the language of subaltern cultures (such as Friulano). The two are integrated and then restated in the author's own social critique which, through literary and filmic production, privileges specific sites (the body of the sub-proletariat, for example) through which to initiate a discourse of subalternity, exclusion, oppression, and confrontation. Though not immune to the seduction and effects of dominant cultural canons, Pasolini's works are an attempt to dissipate the officiality of particular discourses by juxtaposing them to disparate alternative elements.

Accattone (1961) marks Pier Paolo Pasolini's venture into film-making, the author's initiation and exploration of socio-political discourses through visual vocabulary. *Accattone* is the first of many forays in Pasolini's methodology of subaltern cultural synthesis. In that, the first of his films, elements of the dominant cultural code, such as the verses of Dante or the music of Bach, are used as background to the actions and bodies of sub-proletarian characters. These acts of transgression are not easily forgiven by the keepers of traditional cultural codes. As a result, the bodies scripted by Pasolini in his films, and the language that emanates from them, attract the negative attention of the scrupulous defenders of the "common good." Beginning his research among the *ragazzi* of the borgate of Rome and the Neapolitan subaltern culture that had already appeared in his books, Pasolini quickly moves to consider the conditions of Third World populations as parallel representations of a subaltern revolutionary storehouse. Within this context, he develops an analysis of filmic language that aims to complement his other practical and theoretical explorations into written and oral languages. However painfully aware he may be of the distance that separates the various spheres of linguistic expression, Pasolini works toward devising a visual vocabulary through which these parallel realities may at times be congruent.

Consciously addressing a potential diversity of registers, and their value as alternative cultural space and instruments of resistance, Pasolini would seem to touch upon what we now-a-days refer to as postcolonial studies. Almost a decade before his first African film *An African Orestes* (1970), *The Savage Father,* a script located in Africa, sets the ground upon which to approach the unfolding reality of post-colonialism and the concurrent rooting of consumerism in the industrialized world.

Abjuration and Confrontation

While always keen to identify populations in whose hands the undoing of his own bourgeoisie culture may rest, later in his life, Pasolini would critique his own blindness vis-à-vis the overly idealistic representations of subalternity that had populated some of his films. In a series of films which Pasolini himself dubbed his Trilogy of Life, the author's scope was indeed to represent the revolutionary power of sub-proletarian bodies, and highlight their potential through the manipulation of imaginative narratives of tales and fables, *The Decameron* (1970), *Canterbury Tales* (1971), and *Arabian Nights* (1974). In his "Abjuration from The Trilogy of Life" (1975), Pasolini declares that these films were an error in judgment (Pasolini 1976, 71). For those who had known Pasolini and his works, this admission should have come as no surprise; most of his abjuration further demonstrated Pasolini's erraticism. As the following verses from "A Desperate Vitality" (1964, 1996) indicate, Pasolini had very acute sense of what his position in Italy was:

> Death lies not
> in being unable to communicate
> but in the failure to continue being understood. (14)

In his abjuration, Pasolini takes a rather cynical stance through which he claims that the bodies represented in the Trilogy were to have stood in opposition to the subculture of mass media and consumerism. He concluded that those bodies had been doomed long before he made the films, the perpetrator being none other than the famed "economic boom" of the 1960s, a phenomenon that threw Italy into the realm of post-indus-trialism and neo-capitalism. It was in this transition to hyper-nationalism that Pasolini identitifed Italy's cultural and anthropological deterioration. Not one to take "death" lightly, Pasolini developed this "failure" into feigned adaptation and conformism, as in this "Communiqué to ANSA [stylistic choice]" (1971): "I have ceased to be an original poet, it costs freedom: a stylistic system is too exclusive. I have adopted accepted literary schemes to be free. For practical reasons, of course."

However, criticism of his work, and accusations of a nos-talgia for an irretrievable past, continued to be leveled against him. Pasolini's response to those who called for him to deal with the problems of contemporary society, to show a conscience of the present, is the rhetorical abjuration of the Trilogy which in turn sets the stage for his last project: *Salò* (1975).

A loose adaptation of Sade's *120 Days of Sodom*, *Salò* is Pasolini's strategy to revive the last days of fascism at the close of World War II, as an instrument by which to suggest a matrix for contemporary fascism's homogenization and objectification of humanity. The degradation of bodies, their use and abuse, torture, sadism, the corruption of eroticism and sexual relations, are the subjects of *Salò*. Pasolini believed that the fascism that had found fertile ground during the early to mid part of the century had not disappeared but had merely changed form. Consumerism, the new fascism, had, in his opinion, decimated the Italian sub-proletariat and it threatened to decimate the populations of the so-called Third World. Of course, *Salò* was no less susceptible to censorship than his previous works. While Pasolini's early works had been threatening for their portrayal of the pre-revolutionary potential of the sub-proletariat, *Salò* is subversive in its out and out identification of the perverse power of fascism and its lingering effects. That fascism works its spell by insinuating itself as protector of accepted norms, order and clarity is addressed ironically by Pasolini in the previously quoted "Communiqué to ANSA." Freedom through "accepted . . . schemes" is, of course, not freedom at all, and with *Salò* Pasolini succeeds in subverting this statement as well. This he does by giving prominence to the narrative schemes of fascism. By having each set of atrocities prefaced by the narrative voice of the fascist bourgeois captors, Pasolini unveils the inherent violence of that ideology. The scheme in *Salò* is much more direct than in other films and, as the fascist-initiated story-telling degenerates into the subjugation of the unspoken and unspeaking subjects, the "practical reasons" of Pasolini's rhetoric come to light.

One distinction between the Trilogy and *Salò* can be made at the level of communication. The works of the Trilogy still preserve a hope in the dialectic potential of the eroticism of sub-proletarian bodies, as communicative of their condition. *Salò* dismisses any chance for communication through the total objectification of sexuality. The dialectic is wholly disrupted and interjected for the sole function and benefit of the system of consumption that is fascism. Communication, or the lack thereof, defines eroticism and pornography respectively. *Salò* becomes the accusatory finger with which Pasolini links fascism, censorship, and pornography.

The film elicited a negative reaction even from those who had in the past been supportive of Pasolini. Italo Calvino, in "Sade Is Within Us," suggests that "a 'moral' effect can be drawn from Sade only if the 'accusation' keeps its finger pointed not at the others but at ourselves. The 'place of action' can only be in our conscience" (111).

Complaining about how Pasolini was wholly discounting of Sade's intentions in *The 120 Days of Sodom,* and of how poorly that text transfers as a vehicle for the recounting of the last days of fascism in war torn Italy, Calvino suggests that the film-maker was out of touch with the world in which he lived. But Pasolini was painfully aware of his inescapable situation as a privileged bourgeois intellectual in society, and the effect that the maintenance of the *status quo* has on those considered expendable. Calvino's suggestions may in fact be symptomatic of the very loss of diversity in contemporary society, and the conviction that pedagogically we are restricted to the lessons of the dominant culture.

Learning from Failure

Pier Paolo Pasolini wrote *Il padre selvaggio* (The Savage Father) in 1963, during the trial for blasphemy for his film *La ricotta.* Because this script was never made into a film, critics refer to it as an "unrealized" screenplay, which automatically relegates the work to a secondary status. The reasons given for this are of course the trial, and various problems associated with finding financial support for the project. Pasolini himself provides a justification for its non-actualization as a film in a short address that follows the text and precedes the poem "And Africa?" that closes the posthumously published script (Einaudi, 1975):

> The court case against *La ricotta* for blasphemy prevented me from making *Il padre selvaggio.* The pain it gave me — and I

tried to express it in these ingenuous verses of "E l'Africa?"
— still gives me pain. I dedicate the script of *Padre selvaggio*
to the Ministry of Justice and to the judge who condemned
me.

Often referred to by critics as "Pasolini's most ambitious work"
among his meditations on the Third World, *The Savage Father*
holds an integral but not as yet fully appreciated position in his
oeuvre. While it remained a screenplay, *The Savage Father*
reaches beyond the categories of film and script, lying some-
where between them. Written just after his essay "La resistenza
negra" (Black Resistance), the introduction to an anthology of
Black writers published in 1961, *The Savage Father* expands on
what may be Pasolini's most extended theoretical statement
about the Third World. "La resistenza negra" relates Black
resistance to the Italian Resistance to fascism of World War II,
thus establishing for Pasolini an extra determinant in his turn-
ing his gaze toward the Third World. Noting that the resistance
has receded into the past and lost its impact on "our world,"
Pasolini identifies within the Black Resistance the instance for a
permanent revolution: "it does not seem that it will finish as it
has finished here for us . . ." Pasolini's faith in the Black Resistance is based on the belief that there has not been a "split
between resistance and Resistance." In other words, the political
movement for national autonomy and the struggle for social
justice are one and the same.

Contrary to most commentators, I would like to suggest
that it is of little importance that *The Savage Father* was never
produced. Its relevance resides in part most effectively in that
very fact. As a document of ideological pertinence, *The Savage
Father* stands in that ambiguous and contradictory space of
Pasolini's relationship with the *diverso. The Savage Father* signals
the beginning of a research and exploration of form, structure,
and language that Pasolini had begun to discuss in a series of
essays on cinema, "The Cinema of Poetry," written in 1965.
These meditations continued with "The Screenplay as a 'Struc-

ture that Wants to be Another Structure,' (1965) in which the writer/director reflects precisely on the viability of a structure that is neither literary nor cinematic but that "[continuously alludes] to a developing cinematographic work." That essay and *The Savage Father* are representative of Pasolini's considerations of filmic language at that point in time, and of a transition/bridging of literary texts and/to visual texts.

Indicative of Pasolini's concern for a pedagogical relationship with the Third World, *The Savage Father* juxtaposes a European figure in relationship to the inhabitants of an unnamed African country (most likely the Congo, given the historical moment in which the script was written). The story revolves around the arrival of a European teacher in a village to teach a class of young men. It indirectly addresses the presence of neo-colonialism and the cultural resistance of the Africans to both the foreign troops and the colonial educational system (though the new teacher supposedly represents a progressive European presence). In the classroom the resistance is broken down by the teacher's introduction of poetry which, while heightening the pupils' sense of their own culture, also seems to establish a cross-cultural mode of communication. Davidson, the pupil on whom the script concentrates, is enraptured by the introduction of the powerful medium of poetry. As a result, he reaches a moment of self-awareness and awareness of his environment that, while on a visit to his village, causes him to participate in a rebellion against the European forces in residence there. Poetry, it seems, has provided him with a new way to see the world. His actions, while apparently on the threshold of insanity, are a result of his increase engagement of the images of his country and peoples as enabled by the poetic process.

The acquisition of a poetic rapport with one's own culture is exemplary of the Gramscian pedagogic theory that so influenced Pasolini, and which goes to illustrate, within this short text, Pasolini's own critique of pedagogical approaches in general. Poetry provides a link with the student's own experience and short-circuits the relationship with the official culture that originally presents it in the context of the classroom. As an illustration of the need to break with colonial forms and colonized expression, at the beginning of *The Savage Father*, the teacher assigns various compositions to the students, which they complete and return. The resulting essays are a disaster because they are still written under an oppressive force. The themes are unqualifiable: rhetorical thoughts that, having lost their usual form, are even sometimes ungrammatical. "[The teacher] yells at them, telling them that they are no longer under the authority and the rhetoric of the colonialists: 'They are free, free, *they are free!*'" (Pasolini 1999, 13).

The colonial educational system, far from "educating" in the Gramscian sense, in other words initiating a pupil to his own culture, has imposed a rhetorical form that worked effectively to bury the students' personal experiences and any manner in which to express them. Nevertheless, the outsider, an educator who comes ignorant but well-meaning, cannot but become a "savage father" who is potentially destructive for the population he means to educate. The cultural distance that separates the teacher from his students is too great. His substitution of explicit colonial forms with new elements of European "high" culture, which he deems to be relevant to his pupils, is plainly arrogant and bound to fail, and no less colonial in its scope than what he is replacing.

Images are given priority throughout *The Savage Father*. The words *Immagine per immagine* (Image by Image) recur in the descriptions of memories or the workings of the imagination. The phrase *Immagine per immagine* works almost as a panning action across the landscape, and reflects for the reader a process similar to young Davidson's re-acquisition of the conscience of his land and culture. The European teacher, attempting to resolve the undoing of African cultures caused by European colonialists, provides poetry as a pedagogical tool. In the poetry that for the teacher is tied to a sense of aesthetics to which violence is foreign, Davidson finds an inventive potential that is truly liberatory in that it makes possible his rebellion against the Europeans. And it is also this inventive use of poetry that results in making evident the pedagogical distance between Davidson and the teacher. Blind to the truly revolutionary power of poetry and images, the teacher finds these results of its use inexplicable and repulsive:

> In your village, with your father, with your brothers, you betrayed yourself, the one real Davidson in Africa, in the world! Excuse my courage to jest . . . But, at least . . . you forgot that you were a modern man, civil . . . Oh, no, it was not your fault . . . You fell back through the centuries, you gave in. You drugged yourself, you participated in rites that are no longer yours, and they are therefore at guilt.

The conviction that Davidson and his companions have been conditioned by a culture of colonialism, that has made of them "uom[ini] modern[i], civil[i]" (modern men, civil) in all its negative connotations, illustrates the teacher's blindness to his own culture's colonizing tendencies. The teacher does not afford Davidson and his companions the option of "invention," the possibility to write themselves as new subjects between worlds. While unable to fully return to a pre-colonial culture, these young men represent the more interactive reality of culture, and deny the purity of cultural direction required by the teacher.

Juxtaposed to the essay "the screenplay as a structure that wants to be another structure," *The Savage Father* takes on an increased value in Pasolini's work. In the former, Pasolini posits a series of situations regarding the nature of the screenplay. He identifies the screenplay as "the concrete element in the relationship between film and literature," but claims that his interests lie not in exploring the transformation of the text into the "cinematographic work which it presupposes." "What interests me," he goes on to say, "is the moment in which it can be considered an autonomous technique, a work complete and finished in itself" (187). By divorcing the script from the film, Pasolini undermines the script's accepted secondary status to

the "finished" product, the film, a status that is further aggra-
vated if the script in question remains unproduced as a film.
Pasolini accordingly elevates the status and function of the
script by proposing its form as "a choice of narrative technique."

However, even within this "choice," Pasolini stresses that,
in order for the screenplay to maintain its value as a form of
transition (or transformation), it must retain its "continuous
allusion to a developing cinematographic work" (187). To make
of the screenplay simply a form in and of itself would be to
merely insert it within "traditional forms of literary writing." Of
course, as Pasolini himself acknowledges, the critique of this
hybrid form will require its own set of new analytical codes,
ones that recognize both the screenplay's typical aspects and its
autonomy. Approaching a critique of the screenplay with the
tools of conventional literary criticism would in fact deny the
form's occult character, "the allusion to a potential cinematographic work." Pasolini refers to this "element that is not
there," but which must be assumed as part of the critical code
and "ideologically presupposed" as a "desire for form" (188).
The screenplay's tendency to representation in another medium (cinematography) is an integral part of its structure/form.
As such, the reader of a screenplay is given a specific role, which
is to lend a text "a visual completeness which it does not have,
but at which it hints" (189). At this point in his essay Pasolini
gives an account of the process of reading that he expects would
result in approaching a screenplay. I will not go into the language that Pasolini developed for his filmic critique. Here it
should suffice to say that the screenplay and its signs propose
and follow a double path of reading and signification. On the
one hand, the literary, in which the sign leads to the meaning,
and the other, the cinematographic, in which the sign leads to
the film, which leads to the visual sign, which leads to the
meaning. This simplified summary does not do justice to Pasolini's detailed work, but here it is meant only to convey the
fact that for Pasolini himself the screenplay always contains that
other form, which is the visual. "The sign of the screenplay

therefore not only expresses a will of the form to become another above and beyond the form; that is, it captures the form in movement . . . the word of the screenplay is thus, contemporaneously, the sign of two different structures, inasmuch as the meaning that it denotes is double: and it belongs to two languages characterized by different structures" (192-193).

The paradox reveals itself when "we are confronted by an odd fact: the presence of a stylistic system where there is still no defined linguistic system and where the structure is not conscious and scientifically described" (194). While the screenplay is a form that moves toward another form, and its structure moves from literary to cinematographic, the language of transition remains unknown, or not-yet known. Making Pasolini's theoretical writings act upon his artistic works enriches the latter while projecting the former into more of a practical functionality. In folding theory and praxis into each other, works such as *The Savage Father* begin to unveil their transitional value. Beyond its inherent movement from screenplay to film, *The Savage Father* can in fact be read as an analysis of the transition from colonialism to decolonization to a postcolonial condition, for it can certainly be said that colonialism contains a structure that "want to be another structure." The unfolding of the story within the screenplay narrates the passage from colonialism's inheritance to postcolonial condition, and the search for a language through which to express the transition.

Pasolini's answers throughout the book may be less effective and adequate than the screenplay's function as a catalyst for them. Poetry and filmic images are what Pasolini proposes, which are not a problem within themselves. The problematic aspect of the teacher's remedy to colonialism is that it is not much more than a sort of neo-colonialism in the guise of progressive pedagogy. As well-intentioned as he may be, the teacher's language and attitude are blind to a sense of cultural determinism that hinders liberation and emphasizes colonial paradigms.

Because *The Savage Father* represents the struggle for political and cultural independence and for a reassessment of positions it must be acknowledged as an ideologically charged structure of movement and transition, and not merely as a frustrated cinematic effort. Read in parallel to the situation of colonialism, it emphasizes that the structures it discusses require adjustments in themselves and in our perception of them as "structures that want to be other structures." Just as colonialism contains within itself its own end, decolonization and the eventual legitimization and expression of postcolonialism, the screenplay contains its own, the film. While colonialism and the screenplay may or may not become those other structures that they contain, their effectiveness does not depend on the completion of those expectations, but on the creative tension that they create and in our own acknowledgment of the eruptive power of desire.

Pasquale Verdicchio
San Diego

BIBLIOGRAPHY

Calvino, Italo. "Sade Is Within Us" in *Stanford Italian Review: Pier Paolo Pasolini The Poetics of Heresy*, Beverly Allen ed., II, 2, Fall 1982: 107-111.

Ferrero, Adelio. *Il cinema di P. P. Pasolini*. Venezia: Marsilio, 1977.

Pasolini, Pier Paolo. *A Desperate Vitality*. Translated by Pasquale Verdicchio. San Diego: Parentheses Writing Series, 1996.

_____. *Heretical Empiricism*. Edited by Louise K. Barnett; Translated by Ben Lawton and Louise K. Barnett. Bloomington: Indiana University Press, 1988.

_____. "Abiuria della Trilogia della vita" in *Lettere Luterane*. Torino: Einaudi, 1976.

_____. *Il padre selvaggio*. Torino: Einaudi, 1975.